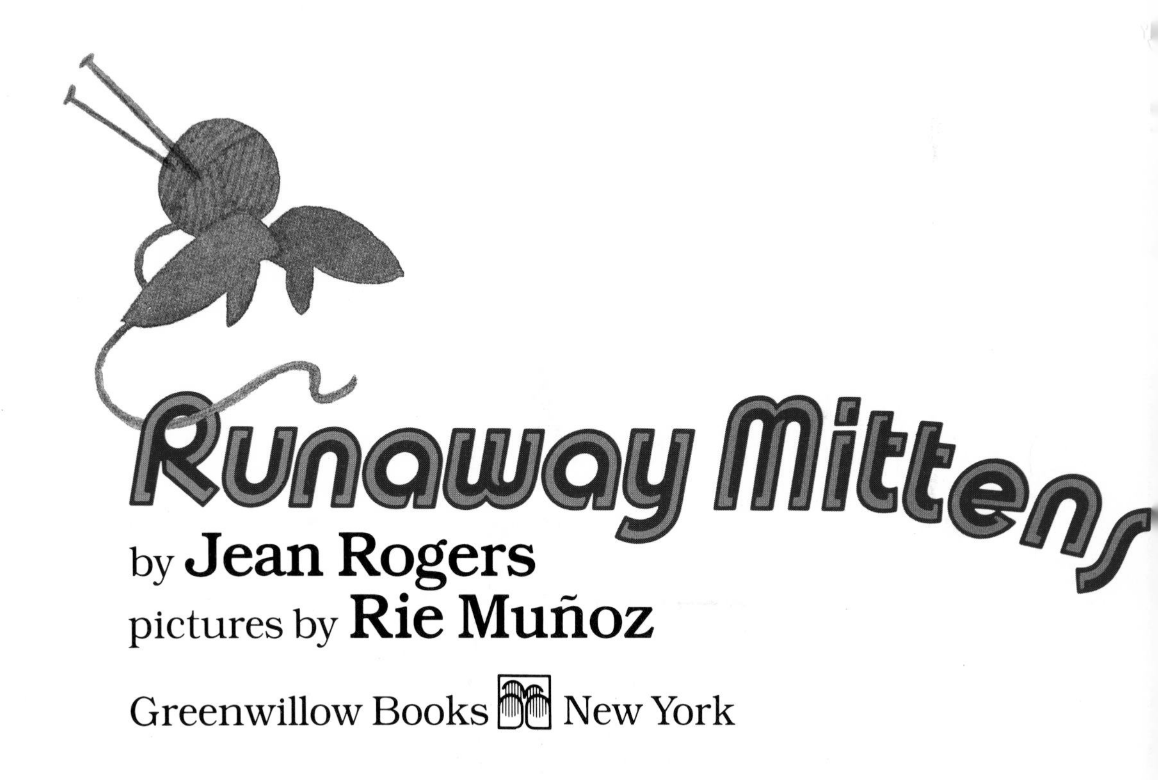

Runaway Mittens

by **Jean Rogers**
pictures by **Rie Muñoz**

Greenwillow Books New York

Watercolors were used for the full-color art.
The text type is ITC Bookman.

Library of Congress Cataloging-in-Publication Data

Rogers, Jean. Runaway mittens.

Summary: Pica's mittens are always turning up in strange places, but when he finds them keeping the newborn puppies warm in their box, he decides to leave them where they are until spring.

1. Eskimos—Juvenile fiction.
2. Indians of North America—Juvenile fiction.
[1. Eskimos—Fiction.
2. Indians of North America—Fiction.
3. Mittens—Fiction] I. Muñoz, Rie, ill. II. Title.
PZ7.R6355Ru 1988 [E] 87-12024
ISBN 0-688-07053-1
ISBN 0-688-07054-X (lib. bdg.)

Printed in Hong Kong by South China Printing Co.
First Edition 1 2 3 4 5 6 7 8 9 10

For Rosemary, the big sister who
could always find the mittens

—J. R.

For Dominic Roussin and Bryan Hamey

—R. M.

Pica's grandmother knit him a pair of bright red mittens. No cold can sneak through the mittens grandmother knits, her stitches are so small and tight and smooth. Pica thinks they are the finest mittens he has ever had.

But those mittens are always getting lost.
"Have you seen my mittens?" Pica says.
"Have your mittens run away again?" Etta asks him. "How is it that my little brother's mittens won't stay in his pocket where they belong?"

Etta is always teasing Pica, but she finds the mittens on a shelf where they were put to dry.
"Mittens," Pica says, "will you please stop running away?"

At school, next day, the teacher says no one can go outside for recess without caps and mittens. "It is too cold and snowy," he says.

"Have you seen my mittens?" Pica asks everyone.

George helps him look. At last Pica spies a bit of red on the floor behind the radiator. His mittens were there all the time, getting warm and dry.

"Come on," George calls to Pica, "let's go or recess will be over."

One day there is a big hole in Pica's mitten.
He takes it to his grandmother.
"I should have made sealskin mittens for my grandson," she says. "With the fur turned inside, your fingers would never feel cold."
"Oh," Pica says quickly, "but these mittens are just right for playing in the snow."

Grandmother smiles at Pica. “You are right. I will get some red yarn and sew up the hole. And when you are old enough to hunt seals and walrus, my grandson, then I will make you some fine sealskin mittens. Now, red wool ones are just right.”

Pica's family is going ice fishing this
Saturday morning.
Everyone is ready to go, except Pica.
"Oh, mittens," he says, "why do you always

disappear just when I need you."
Pica looks everywhere. The mittens are not on the shelf, they are not behind the stove, they are not under the couch.

“What is that bit of red sticking out
of your pocket?” asks his mother.
“You need special glasses made just for
finding runaway mittens,” Etta teases.
“What I need,” Pica answers, “are
mittens that never run away.”

Finally they are ready to fish.

A few days later a big storm comes howling out of the North. The snow swirls in all directions—up, down, around, and about.

Pica and Etta can barely see their way home from school.

Father has brought Pin into the house and fixed her a box by the stove. It is too cold for her to have her pups outside.

There will be no school until
the storm blows over.

The sky is bright blue again. It is so cold and still outside that everything sparkles and crackles. Pica and Etta are getting ready for school.

But where are Pica's mittens? Last night they were safe in his pocket. Now they are nowhere to be found —

not on the shelf,

not behind the stove,

not in his boots.

“Etta!” Pica shouts. “Come and see.
Pin had her puppies last night!”

Etta looks into the box. “Nine little sled dogs with white paws and black noses,” she says. “But what is that red thing under this puppy?”

"My mittens!" Pica shouts. "This time you stay right where you are and help Pin keep her puppies warm."

Pica looks at the wriggling, squirming puppies. "It's all right, Pin," he says softly. "I'll keep my hands in my pockets. Spring will soon be here."